PRAISE FOR MARIA ABRAMS

"I fucking loved this book! Just when I thought I knew where it was headed--I was wrong. And I love to be wrong. A thrilling ride. I want more!"

— ALI SEAY (*GO DOWN HARD)*

SHE

who rules the

DEAD

MARIA ABRAMS

For Dad and Mom, as always.

CONTENTS

CHAPTER 1: AWAKE

THE VAN JOLTS ME AWAKE. It must have hit a pothole which isn't too surprising given that the last time this stretch of highway was maintained was decades ago.

Can you even still call it a highway if cars no longer use it? It was once a congested artery bisecting the country. Until they built one with four lanes, making this one both forgotten and abandoned. A road less traveled indeed.

Despite the bonk of my skull against the window, I try to keep my eyes closed and my body relaxed. Anything to make him think I'm still asleep.

It doesn't work. He knows the impact was too jarring for anyone to sleep through.

"Is your head okay?" he asks.

Instinctively my hand moves upward to feel if any damage was done. My wrist makes it about a centimeter before the bindings stop it. How quickly I forget.

"I guess so," I say dryly, angered I forgot my hands were tied together and that I'm tied up in the first place.

The driver swivels his head. He glosses over me and directs his aim at the window before whipping his head back so that he doesn't have his eyes off the road for too long. Though there hasn't been a single driver on this road for hundreds of miles. Better safe than sorry.

"It's fine," I say to him.

He smiles, contented.

"The window, that is," I add.

His smile falls. It's exactly the response I wanted. The window seems fine. My head left a quarter-sized grease stain, but none of the black paint had chipped off.

"That *is* what you were checking for?" I continue, hoping to salt the wound even more.

He focuses on the road ahead. "I wanted to make sure you were okay," he says.

With everything that he's done to me, to the others, he still wants me to like him. Pathetic.

"You know they sell vans without windows, right?" I ask despite being thankful he didn't opt for one of those. At least I can at least see streaks of desert whooshing by through the more transparent parts. the areas where his paint strokes are thinner. Or did he use a spray can? The ridged ribbons resemble those of a brush, but spray-paint is cheaper. And judging by the quality of the other items in this van, the driver isn't living a life of luxury.

Besides bursts of barren land, the soil white and dried, there's light that pokes through, making the paint glow orange. It helps with the motion sickness.

"I'm aware," he says with a punch. "I already owned this ride. All it needed was a little TLC to work perfectly for what I needed," he says as he gives the dash a gentle, loving caress.

"It was my mother's," he continues as if I care. "She needed a big car for her big family. We would all fight for the prime seats; the ones by the window. The older kids always won. When they grew up and moved out, the next in line would take over the primo spots. Eventually, it was just me. Sitting all alone in this huge thing. I would pretend I was in a giant ship-"

"What does your mother think of you now?" I ask, interrupting him before he gets too deep into his reminiscing. The last thing I want to listen to is him waxing nostalgic about his childhood. Though it might shed some light on when it all went wrong, and I'm curious where the turning point occurred.

Isn't that usually the case? Some childhood trauma that leads to the creation of a monster like him? Or are some people just born bad?

He doesn't answer the question. Not surprising. Instead, he chews on his lower lip.

It's his tick. When he's thinking deeply or frustrated, he chews on his lip. On closer inspection, the pink skin is pocked and scabbed from the indents of his teeth. He's in desperate need of some intense moisturizing balm.

This time, it's because he's thinking. Besides the chewing, it's the way his brows twitch in reaction to the conversation he's having in his head. After a few more twitches, he can take it no longer.

"You should be grateful," he says through clenched teeth. "The others," he takes a breath, "they were not nearly as important as you are."

His hands grip the wheel tighter, the sweat between his palms and the faux leather making a squeak. The whole interior of the van is made of the same material. An artificial plastic-based fabric, that's punctured with holes and cracks from usage.

My wrists are tied behind me, but I can feel the material under my fingertips. With my right hand, I pick at a hole in the seat. It's not an attempt to free myself, it's only a way to direct my emotions. My tick.

I'm awake, but not enough to engage. The drugs are still in my system, and I would love to go back to sleep. No matter how much time I have to think about the way we met, I still can't figure out how he did it.

It's nearly impossible to trick me. I've seen it all, I've done it all, I've heard it, and so on and so on. I also don't get close to people physically. It's a self-imposed rule I do not break. And yet, somehow, this buffoon was able to both sneak chemicals into my drink and escort me out of a public place without anyone paying attention.

Isn't that the way it goes, though? Drunk woman being led out of a bar by a handsome stranger and no one bats an eye. If it's not happening to them, it has no importance.

Humans are the worst.

CHAPTER 2: MISSING PERSONS

NEWS ITEM FROM THE *DAILY CAMERA*:

Search Continues for Missing Boulder Family
    BOULDER COUNTY, Colo.

Monday marks exactly one month since Deborah Jones and her son, Justin Jones, went missing, but officials are still optimistic that more information will lead to a discovery.

The mother and son duo were reported missing by Dave's Diner cook, Tomas Rodriguez, when the pair did not show for their scheduled work shift.

"They've never been late," he told reporters twenty-four hours after making the call. "They're a good family, and I pray wherever they are, they come back safe and alive."

Despite multiple searches and interviews, Deborah

Jones, 45, and Justin Jones, 13, remain classified as missing persons.

In an online press release Sunday afternoon, Boulder County Sheriff Drew Chase issued the following statement:

The news that two of our Boulder citizens have gone missing was a great shock to the community. I can assure each resident that this case has become our top priority. We know that many in our town still feel the effects of the heinous murder that occurred here decades ago which stunned the entire nation.

We at the Boulder County Sheriff's Department with help from other local authorities are confident that the Jones family will be found. Please be assured that we are doing everything in our power to make sure the conclusion of this case will be swift.

The number one priority in our mission statement is valuing human life. We remain dedicated to upholding this promise to both the state and the town of Boulder.

The sheriff's office has also requested to speak with anyone who had communications with either Deborah or Justin to call the tip line, stating "We want to hear from you. Please contact us with any tips whether you feel they are valuable or not. No information will be disregarded."

Naturally, residents in and around the area have growing concerns about the possibility the disappearances are a result of a violent offender. Facebook groups are abuzz, with many posts containing questions about how officials plan to offer protection should the disappearances be officially classified as murders.

One resident, who prefers to remain unnamed, told reporters, "It has been over thirty days since they've gone missing. Everyone knows after forty-eight hours, the chances of being found alive are low. I want to do what they're doing to keep the rest of us safe."

Another poster writes, "They probably just ran off. Have they checked if she owed money to anyone or if she was running from someone? I've heard of situations like this, and a lot of times it is an abusive ex."

A source from the sheriff's office tells us that Deborah Jones had no history of missed payments on any of her loans, nor was she back on rent. Likewise, there is no evidence to point to the disappearance being a result of a previous, unhealthy relationship.

"She always paid on time," says Phil Sommers, her landlord for over six years. "In fact, she was one of the best renters I have ever had. Kept quiet and clean and never tried to sneak in pets. The cottage is going to feel empty without them."

As the school year continues, students at Boulder County High School have been organizing fundraisers and vigils to celebrate a beloved student. Justin's disappearance has had a great effect on many of those who knew him.

"He's one of my best friends," says Cooper Finnegan, a classmate of Justin's. "Justin is like a brother to me. I can't imagine life without him. Justin, if you're out there reading this, we miss you, buddy."

Counselors from the school are ready for drop-in sessions for any students who are feeling affected by the disappearances and are urged to take advantage of all available psychological services.

Last contact with Deborah Jones was made in person at Dave's Diner. She was wearing a Dave's Diner uniform polo and black pants.

Last contact with Justin Jones was also made in person at Dave's Diner. He was also wearing a Dave's Diner uniform polo and black pants.

Please contact Boulder County Sheriff Office with any information about Deborah or Justin Jones.

Subscribe to our newsletter to receive alerts as this story progresses!

CHAPTER 3: JUSTIN

"Your mom's out there, loser," Cooper told him in front of the row of lockers.

Justin rolled his eyes. Seriously, "loser?" Couldn't he do any better than that uninventive nickname? Cooper was as dumb as he was popular.

"She's looking super hot in her tight, little waitress uniform," Chris said, bumping Cooper playfully with his hip. The two boys flanked Justin as he tried to pack up his textbooks.

This exchange was a daily occurrence, one that Justin stopped reacting to. Cooper and Chris couldn't continue with the rest of their days unless they first threw a few jabs at Justin. And every day he took it, packed his backpack, and left, fantasizing about punching the two boys so hard in the face, brain matter would flush from their ears.

But it had to remain a dream. Justin knew that even one negative remark, one act of retaliation on his part, and he would be expelled.

He was the "poor kid," the one who brought down

the school's upper crust, Boulder image. Administration was jumping at the chance to get rid of him which would break his mother's heart.

The bullies became distracted by a gaggle of cute girls by the bathroom door, giving Justin the chance to escape.

The feeling of relief was short-lived. As soon as he saw his mother, hitting the dashboard to fix that mysterious rattle, his heart sank all over again.

Her face was so sunken, her expression so desperate. Justin's thirteen-year-old mind couldn't handle the amalgam of emotions. The sadness, shame, disgust, and guilt all blending into one feeling: anger.

He drew up his hood to avoid eye contact with any other bullies lurking around and sat in the car.

"How was your day?" His mom asked, as she did every damn day. Why couldn't she just drive in silence?

Justin didn't want to talk about his day. About how Mr. Peterson made him take off his sweatshirt, revealing the fact that he wore the same Broncos t-shirt yesterday. It smelled fine and he spritzed it with generic Febreze that morning. No one questioned him for wearing the same hoodie all week, but heaven forbid you repeated a t-shirt.

At least the diner would provide some respite. His mother thought him having a job was a sacrifice. She had no idea how much being at the diner felt like a vacation. There was a comfort in seeing different groups of people rotate in and out, paying him little to no attention. Busboys, like janitors and maids, were invisible to consumers. It was exactly the way he liked it.

His shift went by without any snags. The only strange occurrence was when a customer asked him his name and whether "the dark-haired waitress" was his mom. Customers never spoke to him unless it was to ask for a soda refill. Definitely never a personal question like his name or who were his relatives.

And how did he know that the waitress was his mom? Must have seen them arrive together, he figured. It didn't matter now. The customer was long gone, and it was almost seven o'clock. Time to go home.

"Don't leave without this," Tomas, the chef, told him.

He held out a yellow, plastic bag that Justin couldn't see through, but knew what was inside: a hamburger, no mayo, and a mix of extra fried foods that didn't make it onto people's plates. It wasn't the healthiest diet, but it kept his belly full.

Justin thanked the chef, waved goodbye to his mother, and started his journey home.

His house was a forty-minute walk from the diner but could be cut down by nearly half if he took the trail. It started off as a paved bike path that followed Highway 36 before branching into a dirt path that led him onto his street.

By the time Justin reached the off-roading part of his journey, his burger was devoured, and he was working on a chicken tender that was cold but surprisingly still crunchy. That's when he saw a man.

The sun had set behind the mountains long ago, and the sky was dark. Justin couldn't make out much of the person standing in the brush, but he could tell the shape was tall. Even with night approaching, it wasn't uncommon to see a runner or cyclist finishing their work-out, but this man was no exerciser.

For one, he was standing still and not on the path.

Maybe he has a dog, Justin thought, searching for the shadow of a leash line. But there was none.

The man was also facing him. Directly. Like he had been waiting for Justin this entire time.

Not one to typically become unnerved, Justin quick-ened his pace, clutching the bag of food.

As he walked toward the man, he made sure not to make eye contact. He didn't want the stranger to see him scared.

Justin's pace turned into a light jog by the time he reached the shadow. He was almost past, almost free, when he heard, "Hey, wait!"

Justin didn't pause to respond. He kept moving past.

The man called out again. "Have you seen a dog run by you?"

Justin stopped. It *was* just a dog walker after all. He took a breath and shook his head.

"She's a medium-sized cattle dog. Grey with spots," the man spoke as he approached. "She got off her leash and I can't find her anywhere."

The moon in the sky was no more than a sliver, but its glow hit the man's face, illuminated it like a spotlight.

That's when Justin saw. It was the same person from the diner. The one who asked him his name.

At the diner, the customer hadn't done or said anything specifically worrisome, but the recognition trig-gered Justin into realizing he wasn't safe. This felt wrong. The man shouldn't be here.

Justin turned to run, a full sprint, not a measly jog. He barely made it a few steps before he felt a weight fall on him, planting his body to the ground.

He squirmed, trying to push the man off. His backpack was still strapped to him, and maybe if he shimmied hard enough, the man would lose his hold.

It didn't work. The man was more than twice his size, and his weight alone was heavy enough to keep Justin down, with or without a wagging pack.

The last he felt before the world went black was something hard smack against the back of his head.

How would his mother react when he never came home?

It would break her heart.

CHAPTER 4: THE MEETING

IT WAS BARELY past sunset when we first met. The nights came swiftly here. It only took seconds for the sun to blink off behind the mountains.

I'm not sure what made me stop at that restaurant just outside of Pueblo. The plan was to make it out of Colorado by nightfall, and an unplanned pit stop would have ruined my timeline.

Maybe it was the flickering sign that read Lamplight Restaurant, giving the abandoned Main Street a cool, blue glow. Or maybe it was what the sign was advertising: ½ off well drinks Monday-Friday. Last time I checked my phone, it was Tuesday, and my mouth was watering for a cranberry with vodka.

A well drink to make you well.

The Lamplight called itself a restaurant, but the only actual diners were a wrinkled couple sitting in the corner poking at a meatloaf and mashed potatoes that were somehow the same shade of brown. The only floor staff was one waitress and one bartender, both of whom looked miserable.

Every other patron, all four of them, were seated around the bar. They all looked just as miserable as the employees. What was happening in this town? Maybe it was the food. Eating brown slush would put a frown on my face too.

I brushed off the top of the stool before taking the seat furthest from anyone. It was a drink I was after, not conversation.

Except for the one with the bartender, of course.

"I'll have a vodka cranberry," I told him. Without a response, he turned and began filling a glass tumbler with ice. He seemed offended by my attempt to sanitize my seat before using it. I was no germaphobe, but I didn't want dust on my black jeans. Sue me.

It didn't take long for the hairs on the back of my neck to stand alert.

Women have many innate gifts. Special powers honed from generations of other women who had to be careful to maintain their survival.

One of those gifts is the ability to tell when a man is staring at you with hunger. It's the cold prickle on your skin, the sudden urge to take a scalding shower. You don't even have to see the man to be able to tell that he's targeted you.

It's never a man you *want* to talk to you, either. Those men don't give you a cold sweat with only a stare. It's always the undesirable ones who keep trying no matter how many times they're shot down. If anything, I do envy their tenacity.

As the bartender was finishing his pour – one that was too light for my taste – I knew there was someone watching me. It would only be a matter of moments before he inched his way toward me, taking a seat, and asking me how I was doing.

It didn't play out exactly like I thought. Instead of the "Hey honey, how are you doing tonight?" he surprised me with a "What brings you to this dump?"

I gave him a polite smile that for whatever reason I still felt the need to do. He told me his name was Henry, which I thought odd. He didn't seem like a Henry.

He was younger, early thirties, with a thick head of sandy blonde hair. None of his features were particularly noteworthy, although the combination made him handsome. It pains me to admit that, but it's true.

The name Henry sounded too old-fashioned, too much like a retired accountant. He looked more like a Luke or Jack. No, even better, a Jackson.

Assuming he lied, I also gave him a fake name: Claire. The name had no greater meaning. I thought it sounded nice enough, and it was the first one that came to me.

Claire. I had never been a Claire before, but I would be for at least the duration of one drink.

That was my plan, anyway. One drink and then I'd be on my way. Technically, I did only have one drink before I left, but I didn't leave alone.

"Where are you from?" he asked, knowing I wasn't a local. I stood out because I didn't have the same scowl as everyone else.

I didn't tell him the truth about that either, but I

figured Claire's from Washington, so I told him, "Seattle."

Without needing a return question, he said, "I'm not from around here either. Actually, I am from Colorado, but not from around *here*."

In unison, both of us scan the room, each making silent judgments of the other customers. It was a petty moment, and not the most mature, but it felt nice to share some comradery.

"So what brings you to this seedy little stop?" He asked, leaning in and forcing a glint in his gray eyes.

This is when I knew he was trouble. As it makes me want to gag to admit he was good-looking, it also pains me to admit a part of me was enjoying our repartee up to that point. But when I saw his eyes, deeply looked into them, the façade faded.

He wasn't the kind of bad boy trouble that results in morning whiskey breath and a broken heart. He was *actual* trouble.

There was darkness in those eyes. No matter how hard he tried to be charming, they were lifeless and cold, completely devoid of human emotion.

Evil acts leave effects on the body. Stains. Especially in the eyes. Effects that cannot be forced away no matter how hard you try.

I knew these effects well; I had seen them too many times. I had seen what these men were capable of, and yet, it wasn't enough to make me run.

Maybe it was fate that made me stay. It might have been fate that made me stop the Lamplight in the first place. Or maybe it was boredom or sheer stupidity.

Either way, I stayed.

He was corrupted, but I was curious. So I ordered another drink and settled in.

The Lamplight hadn't been updated since it was built which appeared to be around the 1970s. Its floor was a mosaic of monochrome linoleum, and its walls were wallpapered with a puce green and gold fabric which I never understood. Fabric is absorbent, and the fumes of this restaurant's offerings would fuse for life. As if the smell wasn't already bad enough.

The Lamplight *did* provide a source of conversation even if it became the butt of our jokes.

"What type of vermin do you think the burgers are made out of? Rat or cockroach?"

"Do you think those diners are in their twenties and they look that way because of the toxic fumes in here?"

A few times our quips were overheard by the bartender. It made his pours even lighter, which I didn't mind. Half price meant I could have double the drinks.

It wasn't until the fifth drink that the haze began. I know what you're thinking. Five drinks would put most in a haze, and the rest on the floor. But alcohol doesn't affect me the same as it does others.

Five drinks, even from a generous bartender, wouldn't cause me to sway and see double.

Whatever he put into my Cape Codder worked fast, and before I could call for help, I was out.

When I regained consciousness, I found myself in the van, spread across the back seat. My wrists were tied together with plastic twine that was both sharp and rigid.

The more I struggled, the more it dug in, and it didn't take long for me to stop trying to free myself.

We drove for hours; on top of the time we had already driven while I was drugged. There was no way of knowing where I was or how many miles away from the Lamplight we had traveled.

I was trapped. It would take some time before I learned where I was going and precisely who I was with.

Which brings us here. Driving through some mysterious patch of desert, the drugs finally exiting my system especially after that last micro nap after my head bump.

Am I concussed? I don't think so. I feel less groggy, the fog in my brain is dissipating. That's the opposite of a concussion, right?

"You're awake," Henry says as I bolster myself upward. Based on how prompt his question is, he must be checking on me every few minutes.

Ignoring him, I try and peek out the muddy window. The landscape hasn't changed much. The soil appears sandier, more blindingly white, but that could just be from the sun changing direction.

"See that over there?" Henry asks, pointing toward a mound that's darker than the rest of the dirt surrounding it. It's a distance away, but I see its outline.

"Around there, behind that hill, used to be a camp. It was back in the days of the Wild West. When they built it, it wasn't supposed to be much of anything, mostly there to provide aid to other members of the government passing through, that sort of thing. Stocked with a handful of soldiers biding their time until they could be transferred or retire. But then they recruited some younger members, those with wives and children who were allowed to live with them in the camp.

As you can imagine, with all of the families present, the camp grew in size until it became a bonafide town. It had a one-room school, livestock, gardens, mercantile, the whole kit-n-kaboodle. At its most successful, the population reached nearly one hundred residents.

And then the massacre happened." He stops talking, taking a sip of his soda. I can't tell if he's trying to be dramatic or just thirsty from his monologue.

He puts down his drink into the cupholder, wet from condensation. It's freezing in the van, but the cup still sweats. Funny how that works.

"One night," he continues, "as the residents slept, someone came into their cabins and butchered them. Whoever had done it used a bowie knife. Cut their throats from here to here," Against his own neck, Henry makes a sweeping motion with his finger, pointing from one ear to the other. He's adding pantomime to make his story more vivid. What will come next? Sock puppets?

"You know the strangest part?" he asks rhetorically. "The man, or so it was presumed to be a man, only targeted the women and children. He popped from house to house, only entering the residences where families lived. When he was finished, nearly all of the women and children were killed."

He pauses, hoping I ask about why the mystical, cowboy murderer only targeted the most vulnerable. Or to ask about his identity. But I stay silent.

Giving up on my participation, Henry takes it upon himself to answer the unspoken questions. "No one ever found out who he was, and the only person who saw anyone remotely suspicious was a lower-ranked officer named Franklin. The problem is that Franklin was also known as the town drunk. He claimed the man was close to eight feet tall, covered in, 'scales like a lizard with eyes as glowing as dying embers,' as he put it. So of course his testimony was considered garbage.

"Nor could anyone explain why the men in the camp didn't react as their families were being slaughtered. They were in the same houses as their wives and children, and yet stayed asleep while their loved ones twitched and bled out right beside them."

Henry turns wistful as he delivers that last line. His mouth droops as his face relaxes. This reaction of ecstasy betrays his good guy act; that everything he's done so far is for his betterment and not for gratification.

Did he always enjoy killing? Or was it something he learned to love through experience?

"Why are you telling me this?" I ask, finally speaking. The story would be fun around a campfire, but Henry doesn't seem the type to be concerned about my entertainment.

"Because *that* was a true tragedy. What I'm doing, what I will do, it's a gift. And yet everyone, every single person, will see me as a…"

"Monster," I finish his sentence. He can't bring himself to say the word, to admit his fate. That when the world finds out what he's done, he'll be labeled a freak.

As if on cue, we hit another bump. The curtain behind me – the one that's supposed to conceal the trunk area – flutters, releasing the stench that it was keeping somewhat at bay.

Now that I get another whiff, I'm reminded that the smell was the first thing I noticed when I awoke in the van. They say aromas are so strongly linked to memory because of the proximity of the olfactory bulb to the hippocampus, and I truly hope I won't have to spend a lifetime being reminded of this time with Henry.

Rust with a hint of sweetness. The candy-coated perfume of decay.

Henry either also notices the smell or heard the curtain swish, and he turns his head. "Fuck," he whispers, steering the van onto the shoulder. "I need to fix that," he explains as he gets out of the car.

After a long glance around, making sure no one's on the horizon, Henry unlocks the back door. My head stays pointed forward. I have no interest in seeing what's back there.

It wouldn't make a difference whether or not I saw the bodies with my own eyes. I already know who they are: two men, one woman, and her thirteen-year-old child. Four bodies wedged together so tightly they don't budge.

Four bodies. And I am meant to be the fifth.

CHAPTER 5: DEBORAH

DEBORAH SAT IN HER CAR, smacking the dash. Her Honda was turning twenty years old soon and had recently developed a rattle that came and went as it pleased.

"Can you just stop?" she asked out loud, though she was the only one inside. The thought of an expensive repair job put a pit in her stomach. Between the lack of customers at her waitressing job, and Justin growing out of his shoes every month, a visit to the mechanic was not something she could afford.

Smack! Deborah gave the dash a hard hit, fueled by her visions of being suffocated by bills, and the rattling stopped.

"See, there you go," she told the car lovingly as though showing it affection would stop it from breaking. Hell, if she had to make out with it, she would.

She would do whatever it takes.

The clock read 2:15 and Deborah looked out the window at the school she was parked in front of. The bell would ring soon, releasing a sea of teenagers anxious to escape and start having fun for the day.

Amongst that sea, there would be one teenage boy, head hung low and hood covering most of his face to avoid stares.

Justin hated that his mom picked him up, dressed in her waitressing uniform covered in grease spots. All of the other students either took the bus or were picked up in Audis and Range Rovers. They had a hunter green rust bucket with a dented bumper from when she was rear-ended.

Deborah would tell him that they had as much right to be in that school as everyone else. They lived in the same county and paid the same taxes. It didn't matter that their house was a cramped two-bedroom cottage in the back of their landlord's mini-mansion. The zip code on her mail was the same.

Her words fell on deaf ears. No matter what Deborah said, her son was thirteen and different from the other kids. It was obvious. His clothes weren't new, he didn't have the latest Apple product, and he wasn't able to regale the other students with stories of his latest ski trip.

Nothing, except winning the lottery, would make a change.

The passenger door opened, and Justin sat, clipping his seatbelt. He put his backpack on his lap, hugging it like a security blanket. Another barrier to separate himself from the rest of the world.

"How was your day?" Deborah asked. Every day she asked the same question, and every day received the same response.

"Fine."

There was no more conversation, not even when they reached the diner. Before she could even put the car fully in park, Justin bolted out and ran into the building.

Deborah sighed as she watched him. It was a sight that always put a pit in her stomach: her teenage son getting ready to start an evening shift of busing tables before walking home. Oh how she hated seeing him work – a boy his age should be playing video games with his friends – but the extra money came in handy especially since he was being paid under-the-table.

The worst part was that he never complained. He just put on his Dave's Diner t-shirt, worked hard, and left with a bag of cold, fried dinner the chef slipped him on the side. All without a single gripe as though he knew how much weight his eight bucks an hour had on their family.

Someday she would work her way out of this place. Maybe go back to school. Get a job that didn't leave her smelling of burnt grease. A career. Even if it meant doing double, triple shifts, she didn't care. She would do whatever it takes.

For now, the thoughts had to remain fantasies that prevented her from falling apart. She couldn't make plans right now, there were hungry mouths to feed. Mouths that would hopefully be gracious in the tipping despite the shit food.

"What can I get for you?" she asked her first table, plastering a smile on her face. The man in the booth tipped his menu, revealing his face. He was returning her smile and appeared harmless enough, but there was something off.

It was his eyes, she realized. Shiny but hollow.

"Tell me, what's your favorite dish around here?" He asked, his voice wavering as though trying to contain excitement.

"The water's not bad," she said. It was her rehearsed joke that she used any time that question was asked, but after he burst out in too hard of a laugh, she regretted making it.

"The Rueben sandwich is pretty good," she added, more seriously this time.

He nodded his head, still releasing trails of laughter. "I'll have the Rueben then, Deb-o-rah," he told her as he read the plastic name tag pinned to her top.

Deborah took his menu and turned toward the kitchen. Jeeze, this guy gave her the creeps.

The fact he could unease her was an accomplishment based on some of the problematic clientele she was used to, and she considered pawning him off to a colleague.

Then she spotted Justin, elbow deep in soapy dishwater, and changed her mind. For better or worse, the creeps tended to tip well, and she was in no position to be so flippant with paying customers.

A customer, especially those dining alone, typically spent less than twenty minutes at a table. This wasn't a place where people ordered appetizers or pre-dinner cocktails. They ordered, ate, and left, which was how Deborah liked it. More tables meant more money.

All she had to do was put up with fifteen minutes of this guy and he'd be gone. She could do that. In fact, she's had to do much worse than dealing with an odd patron.

When the Rueben was ready, she brought it over. Reluctantly. He watched her approach, and she could tell he was gearing up to engage in conversation. Had he been rehearsing his words this whole time while waiting for the sandwich?

Such a creep, she thought as she put the plate down.

The man eyed the food and made an overexaggerated *mmm* while rubbing his belly in circles. The Rueben was the best item on the menu, but it was nothing special. Definitely, nothing that warranted such a display.

Deborah nodded politely and pretended that another table needed her urgently. As the man ate, she tried her best to ignore him, not even giving him the customary "How is everything?" midway during the meal.

Had she not been keeping herself purposely occupied on other tasks, she might have seen the man try to engage her son. She would have seen how predatory the exchange seemed. No one ever spoke to her son, and never about anything personal. He was just the busboy, the invisible worker bee who kept tables clean.

If she had seen, she would have rushed the man away and insisted that Justin stay at the diner for the duration of her shift so that she could drive him home. He would have been safe.

But she hadn't seen. She had been too focused on marrying ketchups and slicing lemons that she attached to the edge of glasses.

She let the customer finish, pay, and then breathed a sigh of relief as he left without a peep. She laughed at herself for being so paranoid, so high-strung. Probably a symptom of stress, she assumed. All because she hadn't seen.

Around ten, Deborah finished both her shift and her side work. She said her goodbyes to the kitchen staff and the other servers and began her short drive home.

Justin would be fast asleep by the time she arrived. Even though he was young, a full day of school and a work shift was enough to wipe him out, no matter how persevering he was.

As she entered her home, she made sure to be extra quiet. There was no sense in waking Justin. He should be allowed at least a few hours of rest before having to face his crummy reality for another morning.

I should treat him to a special day, Deborah thought, picturing the places they could visit together. The zoo had a discounted event coming up. Did Justin still like the zoo? He did as a kid, wanting to spend hours in front of the chimpanzee exhibit, but he was older now. No longer a child, but a budding teenager.

Did she still even know him at all?

Feeling that all-too-familiar pang of guilt, Deborah walked toward her son's room. Her plan wasn't to wake him, but just to see him. He was so serene when he slept. If she thought hard enough, maybe some of her loving thoughts could pierce into his dreams. Let him feel carefree for a while even if it were only in his subconscious.

Deborah turned the knob and pushed the door, careful not to make it creak. She peeked inside. The light from Justin's computer charger was bright enough to show the bed. And also to show that it was empty.

No longer concerned about the noise, Deborah flung the door open. She ruffled the comforter as if he were somehow hiding between the folds.

He wasn't there.

Deborah raced through the house. The more places she checked without seeing her son, the more panicked she became. The house wasn't large, and it didn't take long to search every room.

He wasn't there, and there was no indication he had been there at all. No backpack or food wrappers in the trash, the usual detritus he left behind.

Nor was he answering his phone or responding to any texts.

"Justin, you *need* to call me back as soon as you get this!" she yelled into her cell.

I should call 911, she thought, her thoughts frenzied. *No, he's a teenager. Teenagers are rebellious. Fuck! He's just a kid.*

As Deborah unlocked her phone to dial in an emergency, she heard a knock on the door.

It's Justin! He forgot his keys. With a sigh of relief and a nervous chuckle, Deborah opened the door.

"Get ready for a funny story–" she began.

The last word died in her throat. In front of her stood the creep from the diner. Stains that looked inky in the darkness blotted his flannel shirt. She could recognize them instantly: blood. Justin's blood.

The man shoved her back inside and slammed the door behind him. He was so strong, but still she tried to fight. It was no use. It didn't take long before he pinned her down with his knees against her chest, unsheathing the thick knife from his belt.

Deborah's final thoughts, as her neck split open, were of regret. Her one job as a mother was to protect her child. And she had failed.

Except the gloom didn't last long. Before her final breath, she stared the man right into his eyes, boring through with her gaze, and made a silent promise.

She would do whatever it takes.

CHAPTER 6: THE MOTHER CRIES

THE PLASTIC TARPS crinkle as Henry kneels over the bodies to fix the curtain rod that slipped down. It's only slumped an inch, but it's enough for him to become paranoid.

The curtain is hanging off a suspension rod that Henry is unscrewing to add length so that it hangs more securely.

He may be a killer, but he's not much of an engineer, and no matter how much he fiddles with it, the rod isn't staying up.

I almost suggest he staple the curtain to the interior upholstery but stop myself. Is this an early symptom of Stockholm Syndrome? Thinking of ways to make your captor's life easier? Or am I just a constant problem solver?

As he plays with the curtain, the smell gets worse. Each time he moves, his knee bumps a body, releasing a cloud of early rot that had been trapped moments earlier.

The vapors combined with the flapping of the curtain creates a fan that's blowing stink right up my nose.

All four victims are dead, and yet I sense their unrest. They especially hate it when Henry is near, and now that he's touching them, even through the plastic wrap, they're angrier than ever.

"That should do it," Henry announces, proud of himself. The rod is stable, and the curtain hangs straight.

On his backside, he scoots over the bodies to exit the van. One of the plastic sheets gets caught on his cuff button as his wrist slides against the mass. A narrow sliver slices open revealing the skin of the hardening corpse inside.

For the briefest moment, as he draws his arm upward to unhook himself, the skin of Henry's palm touches that of the body below him.

AAARRGGGHH! The mother's scream bullets into my head. My skull feels full of a hundred wasps buzzing and stinging at once. I try to reach up to grab my hair, to rip it out, and yet again forget that I am bound.

The twine digs itself further into my wrists as I writhe in place. As it rubs, it burns, and it's almost enough to refocus my thoughts. Almost.

Her outburst doesn't last long – it's gone by the time Henry frees himself – but the ache lingers.

Henry hears nothing of the screech, of course. All he can hear is my sudden yelp and the sound of my jeans sliding against the cheap vinyl seat.

"Are you okay?" he asks. "What happened?"

"I'm fine," I answer as I lay myself down. My head

throbs like a dull migraine and I'm left exhausted. There's nothing worse than the angry dead. And when that anguish is from a mother, the pain has no bounds.

CHAPTER 7: GEOFFREY

GEOFFREY RUBBED HIS EYES. They were strained from all the squinting. Either the ingredient listings on food packaging were shrinking, or his eyes were getting worse. If it were the latter, it would mean he's getting older, and that wasn't a topic he was yet willing to deal with.

No matter how many times he went food shopping, he couldn't be sure which items had tree nuts, shellfish, or soy and which didn't. Terrance was worth it, though, and the thought of accidentally poisoning his boyfriend still caused concern even after dating and feeding him for over three years.

Satisfied that the can of vegetable soup he held wasn't hiding a sneaky allergen, he put it in his cart. Then he put in four more cans. Might as well stock up on the items he knew were safe. If Terrance didn't like the flavor, he would have to deal with it. Picky eaters can't be picky choosers.

Relax, Geoffrey reminded himself, making sure to ease the tension in his shoulders. Tonight was a special night, and if done properly, maybe the most special night of his life. As long as Terrance said yes to his marriage proposal.

But planning an engagement dinner for someone with such a limited diet was dreadful especially for a self-proclaimed "foodie" such as Geoffrey. When thinking of a proposal, he always imagined a five-star spread: burrata and hamachi crudo for starters, caramelized sea scallops and a dry-aged ribeye for the mains, and for dessert, creme brulee with a platinum ring on the side.

Instead, he would have to settle for a mishmash of courses that Terrance could tolerate because, besides his actual, throat-closing allergies, he had a laundry list of ingredients he could only consume in small doses.

Geoffrey put a bag of chocolate cream cookies in his cart. These would be just for him so he could stress-eat before and after this evening.

"Excuse me." Someone had managed to sneak up to Geoffrey in the aisle while he was pouring over food labels. "Do you know where they keep the sesame seeds?"

Geoffrey let out a chuckle. Thanks to Terrance, he hadn't eaten a sesame seed in years. "You're asking the wrong person," he replied jokingly, "but if I had to guess, it would be with the spices..."

His sentence trailed off before he could also suggest the Asian section. A man, mouth widened in a grin, was standing next to Geoffrey. He was tall, nearly eye level, and wore a jacket and jeans made out of the same shade of denim. Geoffrey and Terrance had a running joke about this type of outfit, calling it a Denver Tuxedo, but this was no time for humor.

There was something *irregular* about the man, something off-putting. Geoffrey couldn't explain why, but the man made him itchy. Maybe it was because the stranger had no cart or basket or anything in his hands. He just stood there, with that devilish smile.

Hoping his recommendation was enough to send the stranger on his way, Geoffrey returned to reading packages.

"I'm making a stir-fry tonight. Need sesame seeds to give it a punch," the man continued, trying to engage Geoffrey in conversation.

It was the way he said, "sesame seeds," barely opening his mouth so that the s's sounded like a hiss. A snake. That's what the man reminded Geoffrey of: a cold-eyed snake full of venom and ready to strike.

Geoffrey gave the man a polite nod and tried harder to bury his face into the row of boxes and cans. *Can't you tell I'm busy, goddamnit?* he thought.

"The only problem is," the stranger continued, "that I'm not much of a cook."

Beginning to grow nervous, Geoffrey snags a box off the shelf too briskly, causing its neighbor to fall to the ground. Both he and the stranger went to pick it up at the same time.

As Geoffrey reached down, he noticed the bottom of the man's pants. On the right cuff were two maroon-colored splotches, noticeable only at that angle.

"Spaghetti sauce," the stranger said, noticing Geoffrey's concern. "Told you I wasn't much of a cook."

Geoffrey wanted to get away. It didn't matter that he wasn't done shopping, he would have to make do with what they already had in their pantry.

Giving up on being polite, Geoffrey turned his cart and pushed it out of the aisle and toward the register without saying another word.

The stranger didn't say anything either, but Geoffrey could tell he was standing there, watching as he departed.

Using a cashier would take too long, and the self-checkout registers were all open. Geoffrey unloaded and bagged each item in rapid succession, not caring if fragile ones were on the bottom. His urge to leave was more important than a broken egg or two. Terrance was probably allergic to those anyway.

Throwing his reusable bags into the cart, he paid and darted out the store.

Why did I choose this *King Soopers?* he asked himself as he pushed his cart through the parking lot. It was a silly question. He knew why he chose this store. It was out of the way from both his law office and the city which meant it was empty. Geoffrey could spend all the time he wanted in each section without worrying about being in the way of other people.

An empty store meant an empty parking lot, and Geoffrey felt exposed as he tried to race to his car. There was only one other vehicle parked next to him: an old van.

Loading the car was even more haphazard, and he heard the clanking of glass bottles hitting each other as he tossed the groceries into the rear of his hatchback.

He didn't hear the automatic doors slide open to let

out a customer. He didn't hear footsteps come up behind him or the unsheathing of a knife. He didn't hear any of these signs of approaching danger.

As Geoffrey reached up to shut the trunk door, someone pushed him down. He fell face-first on his bags. The groceries enveloped him, sucked him down so that he was unable to turn.

He felt a hand snatch the top of his hair and pull his head back so forcefully it gave him whiplash. In a last-ditch effort, Geoffrey clawed through the bags trying to find anything to use as a weapon. Grasping his fingers around one of the soups, he tried swinging his arm backward, but it made no difference.

All he hit was the side of the trunk wall as the blade sliced his throat open.

CHAPTER 8: THE DESERT

THERE'S a high-pitched wailing coming from the distance.

In my woozy state, I worry it's the child. My body tenses. Two blasts in a row would knock me out, even if the child's grief is more subdued than his mother's. He's too young to truly know what he lost: a future.

The wail calls again, and I realize it's coming from an animal. Most likely a coyote. My body relaxes and I open my eyes. Coyotes don't attack unless provoked, and a wild animal is safer to me than the dead.

"You should eat something," Henry says, presenting me with an open bag of beef jerky.

I try to inch back, but my torso is stuck. Once again, I'm taken by surprise at my bindings.

The constraints are more restrictive than before. Henry has me tied to a boulder with the same dense, frayed rope, only more of it. If the rope were new and smoother, I might have been able to slide upward. But it's not. It's also so tightly wrapped, that my thoughts are no more than wishful thinking anyway.

"You need to eat," he urges me, again bringing the mouth of the pouch closer to my face.

"I'm not hungry," I tell him.

"Claire," he says still believing that's my name. "I know you're probably scared and your nerves are shot, but eating will make you feel a little better. I promise."

Shot nerves aren't why I don't want to eat his dried bits of dead flesh, so I ask, "What's the point of eating? You're going to kill me soon anyway."

Henry stops chewing, a line of mucky spit drips from the right side of his mouth. "Suit yourself," he says, returning the pouch to his lap.

It's dark outside, almost deep purple. The only light is a battery-powered camping lantern Henry has set between us. We're in the middle of the desert in some spot he has scouted. Not even a pin of light is visible on the horizon, allowing the stars above us to glow with such intensity I haven't witnessed in a long time.

It's all so close to being beautiful, and as I watch the sky, I come close to allowing myself to enjoy the view. But my dull headache and the sound of Henry grinding the bits of meat between his teeth make it impossible to relax.

"If you're not going to eat, you need to at least drink something." Henry reaches into a plastic bag sitting beside him. Printed on it is a distorted yellow happy face and the words "Have a Nice Day!" which I find ironic.

Out of the bag, Henry takes out a bottle of water, unscrews the cap, and begins crab-walking toward me.

I'm not sure why he doesn't simply stand to make it easier. He doesn't need to be at my level to hand me a bottle.

"If you untie me, I can drink it myself," I tell him before pursing my lips, so he doesn't try and force me to drink.

Henry laughs as though I made a funny joke. "You know I can't do that."

My eyes scan the horizon. "Where am I going to go?" I ask him. "We're in the middle of nowhere."

"I can't take that chance. You're the final piece of the puzzle, Claire. If I lost you now, it would be all over." He inches closer. "You know that."

Apparently, I know a lot.

Henry tries to force another glint in his eyes to seem approachable. His voice is calm but has an underlying edge as though he could explode at any moment. It's the tone of a sociopath: false compassion to hide a bubbling volcano.

It's true that I know a portion of his plans. When I awoke the first time after the Lamplight, Henry treated me to a diatribe.

His speech was supposed to pacify me from kicking and making noise, using the same saccharine voice he puts on when he wants to be soothing. We were still too close to civilization at that point, and he wouldn't be able to explain why there was a bound, frantic woman in the back of his van.

Instead, it reminded me of a true-crime story I once heard on a podcast. One about the serial killer who played a recorded tape as his victims awoke in a basement. That tape, unlike Henry's lecture, was meant to terrify the women, outlining the captor's sick plans for however long he wanted to keep them alive.

Henry took a gentler approach, trying to be encouraging. "You're important" and "your place in the ritual is the most special of all." But the overall feeling was the same: the only real plan this man had for me was murder. I was to be the last cog in a ritual sacrifice.

"You could get someone else for the fifth," I tell him. "Trust me. You don't want me."

"There isn't enough time. And the sacrifices picked *me*, remember? Not the other way around," Henry grunts softly. "Weren't you paying any attention?"

I try to shrug, but the most I can manage is a sad wiggle. "It was hard to stay on track through all the drugs."

The water bottle crinkles under Henry's clenched fist. He bites his lip. "It's alright. I enjoy talking about it."

He stops trying to make me eat and drink and is now swayed by the promise of telling a story. Screwing the cap back onto the bottle, he sets it aside.

Some water squirts on his palm, and he brushes it away on his cargo pants. They're the camping kind that can unzip into shorts. The water forms three lines of wet darkness against the ecru material. A claw mark.

"It wasn't as if I went seeking for all of this," he begins. "I know what they're going to say. That I was crazy and snapped and went on a spree. They'll say that I had a history of childhood violence, ripping wings off of flies. Or sexual abuse. Whatever excuses that will help people sleep at night so that they don't have to think about the existence of that which we cannot see."

Better strap in. This will be a long one, I think, hoping that Henry won't spend the rest of the night in a manic rant.

My head tilts back and rests on the top of the boulder. It's pointed and presses against the soft spot between the base of my skull and the top of my neck. Maybe if I press hard enough, the rock will pierce through. It might make this headache go away at least.

"It all started with a dream," Henry continues, unfazed that I'm staring at the sky and not him, "I'm standing in a wasteland. No plants, no birds, not even a single beetle crawling around, no life whatsoever. The dirt below my feet is red and so is the sky above me. In the distance, I can see a river. Its water is viscous making the flow sluggish like molasses. I can't tell if its color comes from the reflection of the crimson sky or if it's blood.

A voice calls to me, saying my name. It's neither male nor female and somehow whispering and yelling at once. *Henryyyy"* He tries his best impression of an other-worldly voice, but it only comes out raspy.

I press harder against the rock.

"I follow the sound. It leads to a figure standing on the other side of the lake. The figure is made up of swirling smoke shadows, weaving in and out of its body like thread being sewn. The figure lifts an arm, palm facing to the sky, and says to me, *Henrrryyyy, bring me five."*

As Henry poorly imitates the voice yet again, I press

down even harder. The pain splinters through my head like thin fingers wrapping around and squeezing. It feels nice to have fingers again even if they're only sensations.

Henry drinks from his bottle, nearly finishing it in one gulp. The salty jerky has left him parches. The refuel is enough to keep him going.

"I had the dream every night. The same request, over and over and over again. *Bring me the five, bring me the five, bring me the five.* The only change was that the spirit was becoming more frustrated the more I ignored the dream. For whatever reason, it couldn't cross the blood river, and I could sense its anger at being trapped on the other side."

"Finally, I gave up fighting. Whatever this was, it was calling out to me, and I had to help. I had to find out what 'the five' were."

My head lifts from the rock. There's a dot of pain where the stone touched, and I can still feel its coolness. The fingers have let go, but Henry has not.

His story is beginning to interest me, which I did not predict. All this time, I figured Henry was nothing more than a roaming psychopath, picking people off based on some sort of holy fanaticism. Religion can do that to people; make them go mad. I've seen it play out a million times.

But the blood river, the crimson sky, and the figure made of moving shadows. It all sounds too familiar.

"Did you find out who the messenger was?" I ask. In my tone, Henry can tell my interest is genuine, and I almost make out an actual glint in his eyes.

"I did," he says. "But it wasn't easy. I had to surrender. That was the key. Letting go. Allowing myself to accept the message."

"So who was it?" I ask, rephrasing my question to be more direct in hopes of receiving a succinct answer.

Henry laughs and shakes a finger. "Not so fast. First, you need to know how I accepted the message," he says.

So much for being concise.

"The messenger must have sensed I was ready because not even two days went by before I met Deborah."

The mother, I think. The memory of her anguished outcry returns, and with it, the headache. I almost tell him to stop, but I must know who the messenger is.

"The moment I saw her at that diner, I knew. Deborah, with her curly black hair tied tightly in that bun, her round brown eyes surrounded by black circles of stress and exhaustion. She wanted so badly to sleep; I could feel it. And I would be the one to give her that gift."

Henry speaks as though he's retelling a victory. He's so proud of himself. It makes me want to beat the smugness off his face.

"Okay, so you killed Deborah and then the others—"

"Still in such a rush!" Henry interrupts me with a frisky tone. "After Deborah, and I guess her son since he came so soon after, I dreamt of the messenger. The spirit sounded more relaxed like it was relieved I was finally understanding. And I noticed something else. It was closer. It was now able to stand by the edge of the river, nearly touching the flow."

"With each sacrifice, the messenger moved even closer. After the third, it was in the blood. With the fourth, it was nearly across. Once I had the fifth, it would be able to reach me."

"Then what?" I ask. "What would happen once it got across?"

Henry smiles, his expression distant. He's approaching a state of euphoria. "It would give me its power. It and I would be one, and I would finally *be* someone important."

"And what if the messenger is lying?" I ask. My question breezes over Henry, not breaking his chipper disposition like I thought it would.

"It's not," he answers sternly. "I've never been sure of many things in my life, but I am sure that the messenger has chosen me for this purpose."

"It's death magic that you're dealing with. Did you know that?"

"I don't care what it is," he says. The edges of his glee begin fraying. He doesn't know about these matters. It's only been a short while since he's become introduced to the darkness. A touch of education might dissuade him from moving further.

"The dead don't truly die when they take their last breath," I explain, my eyes locked on his. "They first release an energy. Not a soul, nothing like that. But an actual magical energy that can be harnessed. Other kinds of magic have this power. Blood magic, sex magic, earth magic. All of them use the released energies. But death magic is a different beast. Only evil uses the energies of the dead."

"How...how do you know all this?" Henry asks in a near whisper, squeezing his brows together.

This is the moment I could change it all. I could tell him the truth. Put him back on track, turn himself in, and never play around with the darkness ever again.

But I say nothing. The truth might scare him, but it may also strengthen his resolve. It's a chance I cannot take.

He laughs. At me, the dumb look on my face, and with relief. "I'll hand it to you. You nearly had me there." He slaps his knee, the one with the claw stain. "Trying to intimidate me so I let you go. Good one, Claire."

"I mean it. You shouldn't mess with these things," I warn him. "You never know what you're going to release."

He keeps laughing and I abandon my attempt.

Let them never claim I didn't give him a chance.

CHAPTER 9: TERRANCE

THE CELL PHONE that Terrance was charging on the kitchen counter buzzed. It read: Jeffrey with a G, an inside joke that began between him and his partner on their very first date.

No matter how many times he saw the name pop up on his screen, it made him think of that night.

They met the new old-fashioned way: online. At first glance, Geoffrey's profile didn't make him appear as someone Terrance would go for. He was pale, freckled, with a thick head of strawberry blonde hair. But he was tall and broad and good-looking even it was in more of a sexy midwestern sort of way.

Thinking *why not*, Terrance clicked "like" on Geoffrey's profile. He had nothing to lose and his track record with men more his type wasn't working out. Within seconds, he received a notification that his "like" was reciprocated.

The timing was too quick and reeked of desperation,

but it wasn't enough to turn him off, so he began a message exchange.

The night before their first date, Terrance almost decided to ghost. They were planning to have lunch at a Thai restaurant in Denver, and Terrance tried to convince himself of any reason not to show.

He eventually did show, and early at that. When he saw Geoffrey turn the corner and walk down the sidewalk toward him, any reservations he had about the date were gone.

Terrance prided himself on the ability to judge character with a single glance, and Geoffrey didn't need to say a word before Terrance knew he was one of the good ones.

The last few men he dated had an edge about them that Terrance thought he was attracted to. But the edge eventually cut, and what he first thought was sexy and rebellious became unhealthy and toxic.

Geoffrey was different. Terrance felt himself being more and more drawn to him as the date progressed. Lunch turned into a drink at a local bar which turned into dinner which turned into another drink at another bar. The night ended with a passionate but brief kiss and the promise of a second date.

Three years later, they now lived together in a loft in the RiNo district and were browsing animal shelter websites to find a dog to adopt together.

It was perfect.

"Do we have orzo?" Geoffrey asked.

Terrance put the phone on speaker and placed it on the kitchen island. He had a vague idea of where they kept the pasta – Geoffrey was the cook, not him – and began opening cabinet doors.

"It would be in the long, skinny one next to the sink," Geoffrey said either reading Terrance's mind or hearing the clanging of doors.

"No, I don't think so. But we do have a shit ton of rice," Terrance yelled toward the phone.

Geoffrey scoffed. As if rice would be an adequate replacement. "Okay, thanks," he said.

"This is the second time you called about food," Terrance said, putting the phone up to his ear. "Why are you stressing so much?"

As if rehearsed for exactly that question, Geoffrey immediately replied, "Are you really questioning me being obsessed with dinner?"

"Who *me*? What was I thinking? Of course not," Terrance said, overexaggerating being offended, even putting his hand on his chest to sell the performance.

Thanking Terrance for his help, and promising he'd be home soon, Geoffrey hung up. The exchange left Terrance questioning Geoffrey's motives.

Geoffrey, bless him, wasn't the most subtle and carried his emotions not only on his sleeve but the rest of his shirt. He sounded nervous on the phone. And this many calls about dinner was a lot even for Geoffrey.

Could tonight be the night he proposed? They *had* been together for a while now, and like any modern couple, previously spoke about the possibility of marriage. It was a notion that excited Terrance, but he didn't want to let himself get carried away. If he expected a proposal and only got dinner, the disappointment would be palpable.

But there was no denying tonight felt different. Anticipation was in the air, and Terrance knew he had to occupy himself from over-thinking.

Deciding he would make the apartment presentable, he spent the next hour and a half reorganizing knick-knacks and lighting candles. The couple kept the apartment well-maintained, so there wasn't much to do in the way of actual cleaning, but Terrance was able to burn a few minutes choosing a bottle of wine for the evening. Or maybe the night called for a cocktail. A custom cocktail. One they could later serve at the wedding as a nod to the night they became engaged.

So much for not getting carried away, Terrance, he told himself, booting up the laptop to search for mixed drink recipes.

He bookmarked a few promising ones and went to their bar area to take an inventory of their alcohol. A Southside Fizz would be nothing without gin, and he couldn't remember if it was gin they were out of or vermouth.

As Terrance sorted through bottles, he heard a knock on the door.

"Coming, Geoffrey," he announced, assuming it was his boyfriend – perhaps soon-to-be fiancé – with an armful of grocery bags, unable to open the door. Besides, who came over unannounced anymore? Their building was only accessible by a key fob, which meant no solicitors or those scammers trying to sell fake magazine subscriptions.

Comfortable that it was Geoffrey, Terrance didn't inspect the peephole before turning the lock. He didn't see that behind the door wasn't his partner, but a killer with an expression of happy surprise that he didn't have to use his story of why he needed to come in.

Terrance didn't see it coming. Not that it would have made much difference. He wasn't a fighter and his slender, 5'8" stature paled in comparison to the lumberjack before him.

All Terrance heard was the door slam shut, and heavy feet running up behind him.

His death was the quickest. Terrance was the only one to not even see his murderer's face. Henry was too excited to take his time. After this one, he only needed one more for it to be complete.

CHAPTER 10: THE STOP

WE SLEEP OUTSIDE. The temperature doesn't dip below seventy, even in the desert. It's a balmy night to top off a balmy day. I don't sleep easily, unless I'm drugged or blasted by the dead apparently, but I especially can't sleep in the heat. Nor can I sleep sitting up, and Henry still has me tied to this fucking rock.

All that's left to do is watch him. The lantern has long gone out, but my eyes have adjusted to the night. Henry is curled up under a hunter-green sleeping bag. The blanket he so graciously offered me – that I so rudely refused – is piled in a ball next to him.

I imagine a baseball-sized spider, its eight bulging eyes and spindly legs, crawling into that blanket only to attack Henry's face in the morning. The spider is venomous, of course, and its poisoned bite begins rotting Henry's face, bits of necrotic skin falling off in chunks as he collapses into a headless lump.

It'll be a story I'll think about later on. It's not every day you encounter a creature that could melt a face off so rapidly. I'll Google the spider later. It'll be called brown-desert-something-or-other. I'll say, "Oh, how interesting," and check my email or a subreddit. And then I won't think about it for a long while.

The fantasy brings a smile to my face. I've begun to hate Henry. Not only because he's kidnapped me with murderous intent, though that would be enough for most. I hate him because he thinks he's special. Some sort of chosen prophet. When in reality, he's a pawn. A nothing little chess piece being moved around the board by a much more powerful hand.

For now, I'll let him sleep. Whatever monster he's in cahoots with shouldn't be my business, anyway. I should end this whole charade now, but I want to see the smug looks get blown off his face when he realizes what's happening.

Whether it's by the bite from a spider or something else.

STATEMENT BY SHERIFF LARRY AHUMADA:

The Ector County Sheriff's Office continues to dedicate its resources to apprehending the individuals responsible for the murder of fifteen-year-old Anna Vasquez.

On Sunday, February 22, at approximately 8:50 in the morning, Ms. Vasquez's body was discovered in a field near Essex Avenue in the city of Odessa. Autopsy reports concluded that Ms. Vasquez was a victim of violent and sexual assault before being manually strangled, which was ruled as the cause of her death.

Detectives from our Major Crimes Division immediately began their investigations into the murder, and thanks to the help of eyewitness reports and the cooperation of the

Odessa City Police Department, were able to identify the perpetrators.

We believe the two individuals responsible are forty-one-year-old Calvin Sweeney and thirty-seven-year-old, Roy Unger, both last seen with Ms. Velasquez on February 20 at Leo's Billiards Hall near the location where the body was discovered.

During our interviews with eyewitnesses, the pair appeared highly intoxicated and possibly under the influence of drugs. They were also seen carrying firearms and are likely armed and dangerous. Extreme caution is advised if the two are spotted.

Further investigations with the assistance of the Texas Bureau of Investigation, showed that Sweeney and Unger have a history of criminal acts and may be responsible for an additional number of unsolved murders in the state of Texas. However, these investigations are still ongoing, and no final conclusions have been made.

We will post photos of Calvin Sweeney and Roy Unger on our website and through our social media accounts. If you have any leads or information about these two, please contact our offices immediately. Again, Sweeney and Unger are considered armed and dangerous and be advised to use caution if approached.

CHAPTER 12: BERSERK

HENRY AWAKES the moment the sun rises. It must be around six. I watch him rub the crusts off his eyes and stretch. Even with a sleeping bag, the dirt ground is hard, and his sleep could not have been comfortable.

I, too, am uncomfortable from hours spent sitting upright. A good stretch seems euphoric, and I almost look forward to returning to the van.

But I have to wait. Henry takes a piss, brushes his teeth with the rest of the bottled water, and unties me after he's already packed up. He doesn't untie my wrists, and they're becoming bruised. The swelling makes the restraints even tighter, and I fantasize about dipping them in a bucket of ice water.

We begin our journey, and as Henry drives, I notice a smirk on his face as wide as the Rockies. He sees me watching, and exclaims, "Today's the day!"

"Can't wait," I respond, under my breath.

He hears me and shakes his head. "I have to hand it

to you, Claire. You're the only one who hasn't been scared. Why is that?" he asks.

He's right. I'm not afraid.

No wait, that's a lie. I'm afraid of what forces Henry is messing around with, but I'm not afraid of him.

"I don't fear death," I say. The answer pleases him.

"As you shouldn't! Especially not in your situation. Your death will live on. Have meaning," he says.

"If I'm so important, then what were the others?" I ask. "Nothing more than steppingstones?"

"Of course not. They all served a specific purpose. Their importance will not be forgotten."

Henry's words sound empty. His false sentiment isn't enough to calm my offense. He's so insolent about his thoughts of the pile of bodies behind me, not resting in peace. Rarely do I feel a connection with the dead to warrant my feelings of disrespect, and I question what's different about these four?

It's likely because I've been trapped near them for so long, absorbing their air. The same air they're not breathing. Or perhaps it was the mother's cry. A wisp of ache still lingers in my head.

"Shit, we need gas," Henry tells me, disappointed in his mistake. There should have been enough gas cans in the back to take us to our destination without having to stop. But the needle is hugging the E, and we're still miles away.

The other problem is that we're still in the middle of nowhere. The last semblance of humanity was an abandoned rock and mineral shop I had spotted two hours ago.

I can tell Henry is stressed. His upbeat demeanor has faded, but he's just as animated.

"Shit, shit, shit," he mutters to himself, his foot pumping up and down on the gas pedal. Should he slow down to conserve fuel or go faster to find a station? He can't decide.

"Turn around and see if there's a spare can back there," he demands.

"I can't see through the curtain," I tell him.

"Push it back with your head. From the side there." He points to the edge of the material.

I twist my body to face backward and push my head past the drapes. Somehow there's enough light coming in even without windows.

It's my first time seeing Henry's collection, and it's exactly what I imagined. Stiffened masses that are beginning to curl, piled haphazardly on one another. They remind me of worms that have dried out in the sun as they tried to crawl across the sidewalk.

The plastic Henry wrapped them in is loose and patchy. Bands of duct tape are wrapped in certain places, keeping the limbs from spreading, although, at this point in the decay process, it's unnecessary.

The mother is laying on top. There's a hairline tear where her shoulder is. I can see a snippet of graying flesh poking through, and it makes me shudder. What I don't see are any full gas cans.

"No cans," I tell him.

Henry hits the steering wheel with the bottom of his palm. "Crawl back there and check. There might be a spare can shoved underneath one of them."

"Absolutely fucking not," I say. There's no way I'm going to risk being closer to the bodies. Hearing the mother's cry was bad enough when it was through Henry, but I can't imagine what would happen if I touched her myself.

"Do it!" he yells. It's the first time I hear Henry angry. He's been on the verge before but has never yelled. "I can't do it myself. Stopping the car will waste too much gas."

"My legs and wrists are tied. How exactly am I supposed to crawl back there?"

"I don't know! Like an inchworm. I don't care how you do it, just do it," he demands.

The image of me wiggling around back there gives me a chuckle, as well as the thought that I would do it. The audacity of Henry's request is worthy of a laugh.

Henry spots my expression of gleeful disbelief, and he stomps on the brake sending me flying against the passenger seat. It doesn't hurt. The seats are cushioned enough to pad my impact. If anything, it makes me laugh even more at how fragile Henry is.

Hoisting myself back onto the seat, I tell Henry, "I guess your plan isn't going to work, Henry."

Henry points a finger in front of him. "Think again," he says as we pass a sign that reads: Food, Fuel, and Friendly Faces! Only 5 miles. The words are hand-painted and cracked from the harsh sun. It will be a miracle if the place is still open, though a miracle is precisely what Henry thinks it is. "Talk about divine intervention," he hoots.

Even if the van runs out of gas this very minute, five

miles is walkable. Gone are any hopes of us breaking down and watching Henry shrivel like a raisin from the heat. Or one of those road-crossing worms.

Unless, of course, there is no rest stop.

Henry opts for the speed approach, and five miles go by in a flash. The gas station can be seen from a distance, and much to my surprise, it's not as derelict as I pictured.

Before we drive up to the pump, Henry swerves off to the side and puts the van in park.

"Now, you need to listen to me, Claire," he orders, a finger pointing at my face as though I'm being scolded by a parent. "Not a sound from you. And don't try anything stupid. The doors are locked from the outside, so there will be no trying to leave. Got it?"

I turn my attention to the door beside me. Henry must have rigged them like a cop car, you can get in, but you can't get out. Guess he's more of an engineer than I thought.

He doesn't wait for a response and cruises into the gas station. There are two pumps, facing opposite directions, and Henry makes sure to choose the one furthest from the shop. The shop is no more than a trailer-sized shack, but there are people visible inside.

Henry leaves the van to begin pumping. He quickly realizes that none of the pumps have a credit card slot, which means he'll have to go inside to pay with cash. Which means he has to leave me alone.

I see his gaze try to meet mine to give me a silent, "Watch yourself." He can't tell me these words out loud. It would reveal there's someone in the van, behind those blackened windows.

Henry disappears into the shop. It's the first time I've been alone for days. Well, mostly alone if you don't count the road trip crew behind me.

Solitude is what I'm used to, and what I prefer. That doesn't mean there's no room for the living once in a while, I do occasionally get bored. But it's isolation I prefer, being lost in my own thoughts with no one to answer to.

As I sit, embracing the quiet, I consider my next move. This charade is reaching its end. I'll need to finish things, but first, I'll see how these events play out. I'll allow Henry to take me to wherever he's going and wrap everything up then.

Content with my plan, and grateful that I had time to think, I rest my head against the window. As I stare ahead, the corner of my view catches something interesting. A crack. A shattered line in the glass, splintering like a bolt of lightning. Exactly where I had hit my head the day before.

It must be chipped spray paint, I think, but as I inspect it closer, I can see glittering from the reflecting sunlight. It's definitely the glass, I realize, and as I do, I hear another scream.

ARGHHHHHH!

It's not as intense as the first time the mother screeched, but it's close. Too close. I can't stand another blast, nor do I have to. I don't need to be here, trapped in this coffin. Adrenaline rushes through me, and I lean back, donkey-kicking my two feet into the window.

The crack grows, I can hear it crinkle as it splits. I kick again. More crinkling, more splitting. One final kick.

With this last effort, my feet go through the window, sending shards of glass flying onto the sandy ground.

I use my bound feet as one, knocking off as much window that's leftover, before I slide my body through, feet first, using another kick for momentum.

My attempts at cleaning the hole aren't good enough, and I end up slicing my lower back. The damage will have to wait to be inspected. However bad the wound is, it's deep enough to leave droplets of blood behind me as I hop. It's difficult to gain distance and I feel like a contestant in a county fair. It beats the alternative: inch worming. Even if that approach saves time, I won't fucking do it.

Finally, I make it to the door and use the force of my body to pop it open. It causes me to fall flat, but I'm inside.

"Help me!" I call to whoever's listening.

When I look up, three faces are looking down at me. Two of them are confused, while one is horrified. My attention moves to the bearded men, both behind the counter.

"He's trying to kill me!" I yell to them, trying to milk the narrative of a helpless woman on the edge of danger. I must say that my performance is exceptional. Thanks to all of the Scream Queens that have come before me.

One of the bearded men realizes what's happening and withdrawals a shotgun he had in arm's distance. A moment as this is what he's been waiting for. It's the reason why every night, he makes sure there are two shells properly loaded. Well, he imagined a cop was a more likely scenario, but this was close enough.

"What the hell's goin' on here?" the man asks, pointing the gun at Henry's chest.

Instinctively, Henry puts up his arms. "This isn't what it looks like," he explains with a shaky smile.

I've propped myself against the front of the counter which is nothing more than a collection of plywood sheets nailed together into a general box shape. The counter isn't the only piece that's makeshift. As I take notice of the shop, I see that it's in even worse condition than I imagined.

Broken wooden shelves line the walls, holding no more than a scattering of dusty cups, magazines, and moldy cardboard boxes. The one floor-shelf that spans the tiny space has a few cans of food, but the lids are off, and they seem to have been emptied long ago.

There's too much debris, too much dilapidation. The place is too rundown even for a secluded road stop as this. It smells too much like piss and shit and body odor.

When I notice the stained sleeping bags in the corner, I know something's wrong.

Henry's still waving his hands in the air and pleading for the two men to hear him out.

The other bearded man, the one without a gun, is still dumbfounded. I'm not sure he's figured anything out. In his defense, neither have I.

"Shut up," the armed man instructs Henry who's started to repeat himself. The man walks over to where I'm sitting and squats down, the gun still aimed at Henry.

"Are you alright, Miss?" He asks me. I hate being called Miss, but now's not the time.

Wide-eyed, I shake my head.

"She's bleeding," says the other man. He's just noticed the red trail that I brought inside. "I don't like this, Cal. Not one bit."

Without averting his gaze away from Henry, Cal asks me, "Did this man hurt you, Miss?"

Again with the Miss, I think. "Yes," I respond, meekly.

"We need to take care of this, Cal," the other man says.

"Relax. I got this," Cal tells him. "Here," he motions for Cal to come over, "take this and keep it pointed at him." Cal hands over the shotgun. It's a smooth exchange, and it gives Henry no time to react before there's already another finger on the trigger.

"Don't shoot him!" Cal barks. "Not yet," he adds, sending a wave of anxiety into Henry's disposition.

The tables have turned, and it's clear that Henry has become the prey.

Cal reaches out an arm and I convulse and slide to the side. There's no room for me to go anywhere. Cal's broad and so close to me that I can smell his whiskey breath.

"Don't touch me!" I shout, no longer acting.

"It's alright. You're safe now," Cal tried to assure me, his arm lifted.

"No! Don't fucking touch me."

After my order, there's a change in Cal's expression. He switches from caring machismo to contempt in a split second. Fed up with my demands, his arms punch forward and he tightly clutches my shoulder.

As I feel the roughness of his calloused palm against my skin, everything becomes clear.

It all happens so fast. Years of violent acts combining into an amalgam of filth that flashes before me. All of the victims were girls, young girls, the oldest no more than nineteen.

The entire slideshow lasts a fraction of a second but contains every murder. I can only see the experiences of the victims who died, their emotions moments before their deaths. I feel their wounds, their bruises, the damage the men caused before ending their lives.

How many others were there? Others that didn't die, that I couldn't see? Bastards like Cal and his accomplice didn't begin with murder. They practice first with the unlucky few who had to continue living with the trauma.

I've only experienced this a few times in the past, but it has been ages. I've become more careful not to touch or be touched, and the number of blood-thirsty rulers has diminished, at least in this country.

This lack of exposure, lack of practice, means I lose control.

I feel fire burst through my body. It starts in the stomach and erupts like a torrent of uncontrollable pain and anger. My legs, feet, arms, hands, and then head roars with energy.

From the outside, I resemble a fiend. My eyes a milky white with threads of black, my skin a road map of protruding purple arteries. The muscles in my body spasm causing me to contort in hideous ways. Ways a human body shouldn't be able to bend.

The constraints hold during my thrashing, so as I stop moving and rise, my body is pencil straight.

This is who I am. It's not my true form. I can control whether or not I shed the human skin. But you can see hints of it under the skin, trying to break out, patches of blackening skin pulsating and stretching. The souls wanting to tear their way out.

Henry's mouth is open in an O, his arms are still pointed toward the ceiling.

"Kill them," I say to him, millions of voices combining into a single boom. "Kill them all!"

Able to shake himself from his stupor at a rapid speed that I'm almost proud of, Henry snatches the gun from the stunned man.

He begins firing, but his aim is unsteady, and the first blast only hits the man's leg. It does push him back, but unfortunately closer to the back of the counter where he takes hold of a pistol. Of course, these two don't only have one firearm. Their IQs may be in the low double digits, but when it comes to bloodshed, they're not stupid.

Henry's in trouble.

Cal has run to the other side of the store, most likely to grab another gun. I'm blocking the front door, and both men are far too terrified to come near me.

I bend forward in a sharp angle and lay the side of my cheek against the floor. It's made of wooden planks that have weathered and chipped from neglect. The wood was once alive but is now dead.

And I am the ruler of dead things.

It's a little trick that's only successful when I'm in this mode. Energy I shoot from my skin discharges through the wood like an electric shock. It hits Cal and his partner, instantly subduing them.

To the pair, it feels as though they've stepped into a pool of electric eels. They have no idea what hit them.

Henry has free reign now. He presses the mouth of the shotgun against the second man's face, not taking any chances with being too far away, and pulls the trigger.

The blast explodes, and the man's head bursts like a balloon filled with meat and fluid. It reminds me of one of those water gun games at the carnival. Point the spray into the clown's mouth to inflate the balloon. The first one to pop is the winner!

On the other side of the shop, Cal is frozen mid-squat, his hand inside of a worn duffel bag. Henry approaches him from behind. It's a predatory stalking motion that he's used to by now.

Cal can't see behind him nor can he turn around. But he heard the blast and knows Henry's coming for him.

A pitiful moan escapes Cal's mouth and Henry uses the gun to push him down.

"I want you to see," Henry tells him, pointing the weapon above Cal's nose before firing.

Cal suffers the same fate as his partner, his now headless body flat against the ground.

The voices of the dead quiet, happy with the outcome.

CHAPTER 13: TRANSCRIPT

Transcript of the press interview conducted by U.S. Marshal Rick Matthews on 8/16/2020 at the San Diego, California branch. Property of the United States Marshal Service.

RM: At 7:42 A.M., the U.S. Marshal office in coordination with the FBI, tracked down Calvin Sweeney and Roy Unger near the town of Chambless, California. The search for Sweeney and Unger began approximately six months ago, after the discovery of the body of Anna Vasquez near the town of Odessa, Texas.

Based upon those initial investigations, it was discovered that Unger and Sweeney are also responsible for the deaths of Laura Bancroft, aged eighteen, Rebecca Jones, aged nineteen, and Rachel Jones, no relation, aged sixteen.

After arriving at the scene, the fugitives were found deceased, thus concluding the manhunt.

Details of the investigation are still being made official, and so I cannot comment on specifics; however, I will now open up the floor to questions.

Reporter 1: Marshal Matthews, can you comment on the cause of death for Unger and Sweeney?

RM: The cause of death seems to be the result of gunshot wounds to the head.

Reporter 3: Was it a suicide?

RM: At this time, the evidence does not point to a suicide. The trajectory of the bullets and blood spatter analysis are not consistent with a self-inflicted shot. We believe there may have been some involvement from a third party.

Reporter 2: Do you believe the third party was an accomplice of the two men?

RM: We do not. There has been no previous evidence linking them to an accomplice. We believe the third party may have been a potential victim that was able to fight back.

Reporter 1: Did the trail of blood belong to one of the two men?

RM: If you're referring to the blood that was found between the gas pumps and the interior of the building, then no, we do not believe it belonged to Sweeney or Unger.

Reporter 1: Was the blood tested?

RM: The blood was tested, and results were inconclusive; however, we believe that it most likely belongs to a female between the ages of thirty and thirty-five.

Reporter 3: Can you speak about why multiple labs had to be used to test the blood and the rumors about evidence tampering?

RM: To answer your second question first, there is absolutely no evidence of tampering with any of the blood samples collected. The rumor, which is all it is, was a result of complications our initial labs had with the tests. The results could not narrow a blood type, and in fact, one error was that each blood type was present in the sample. A similar error occurred when trying to narrow age and sex with results ranging from all ages and sexes.

Reporter 1: Do you have any leads on the possible location of this third party?

RM: At this time, we do not; however, we are beginning to narrow areas that we believe the third party may be located.

Thank you all for your time. Unfortunately, I cannot take any more questions. We will provide another update when more information becomes available.

CHAPTER 14: HENRY'S HOUSE

SEVEN DAYS HAVE COME and gone since we've arrived at Henry's house. Maybe more, maybe less, I can't be sure. There are no windows in the basement, so there's no way to count sunrises and sunsets.

The only light I have is the utility light that's no more than a bulb fixed to the ceiling. Plus, it only goes on when Henry comes downstairs for a visit.

His visits are frequent and always annoying. At this point, I'd prefer sitting in the dark than listen to his incessant questioning. My refusal to play along means nothing to him. The questions don't stop. He has a captive audience. Literally.

My wrists and legs are still bound, except I've received an upgrade. Gone are the plastic ropes with the sandpaper edges that bore into me. They've been replaced with metal chains, their coolness a welcome relief against the rawness of my wounds.

The chains that tie my limbs together are connected to more chains that lead to a cinder block wall. Screwed into the wall is one large steel loop that holds the attached chains.

The entire contraption forms a web of woven metal with me, smack dab in the middle. I feel like a trapped fly waiting for the spider to approach.

Too bad the spider is no more than Henry. He's overjoyed with his newest acquisition. He thinks he's won. It's not in the way he had planned, but he's too ecstatic to question the disconnect.

The reality of this situation doesn't match with the messages in his dreams. There was no fifth sacrifice, no final act of devotion in order to invoke whatever spirit was trying to commune with him.

Henry is convinced *I* am that spirit.

Who am I? I'm not the one who spoke to Henry. Entering people's subconscious through cryptic visions isn't my M.O. It's tacky and frankly unoriginal. Save that nonsense for the straight-to-DVD horror movies with the bad cover art.

My approach is more direct. Like losing my mind in an abandoned rest stop and initiating the slaughter of two men, even though they deserved it.

Who am I, then? Better yet, *what* am I? Some call me a demon, others an angel. I'm neither and both: not good nor evil. I'm supposed to be an impartial protector of the dead. A representative, so to speak. Notice I use the term "supposed to."

My anger is causing me to sway toward the side of darkness. The incident at the rest stop is more indication that when I lose control, my first thought is to destroy. I want to take away their life force and lead them to an eternity of punishment. It's not my place to cast that kind of eternal judgment, and yet I've been doing so more and more.

Sitting in this dank, lightless room has given me time to reflect. Except when Henry interrupts me. Like he's about to do now.

The locks on the door to the basement are being opened. Henry marches down the stairs and tugs the hanging chain to turn on the light.

The room is as it has been: musty and dank stone, dotted with patches of mold. The only architectural detail is the rusty pipes that crisscross the ceiling like a subway map. Those pipes are also my only source of sound. I hear the water flow, shaking the PVC lines causing them to hammer. It helps drown out the whispers of the dead.

Henry approaches, holding a plate of food: French fries and a pile of green mush. "I brought you something to eat in case you're hungry yet," he tells me, placing the plate on the ground in front of me. It's close enough that I can reach if I want to, but far enough that he doesn't have to come near me.

Henry is fascinated by me, but he's equally as terrified. He's witnessed a fraction of my talents, and he can only imagine what other powers lie beneath.

I'm not interested in the meal.

"It's fries and sauteed kale," he explains. At least it's not meat, for once. Henry's diet seems to revolve around burgers, beef jerky, and chicken tenders that he microwaves. It's a miracle his heart hasn't stopped, but I'll give it ten more years. Ha! As if he'll make it that long.

"I'm going to save you from having to keep trying to feed me. I don't need to eat," I tell him, hoping to reduce the number of times he visits.

"Why is that?" he asks, leaning a bit closer in genuine curiosity. "Is there anything you *do* eat?" He leans closer still. "Do you eat souls?" he says in a whisper.

Figuratively, yes. For sustenance, gross. But all I say is a flat "No."

"I saw a vampire movie once where the vampires would get violently sick if they ate human food. Throwing up blood and vomit, all that good stuff. Will that happen to you if you eat this?" He asks, pointing to the food that's now grown cold. "Will it harm you? Will you puke out blood?"

What's with this guy? It's one stupid question after the other. No matter how many one or zero-word answers I give him, he keeps firing at me.

"No," I repeat in the same monotone.

Henry sits on the floor and crosses his legs. Looks like he's planning to stay awhile.

"You drank at the bar when we met," he says, remembering our first time together. "So I guess you can drink, but you haven't drunk any of the water I gave you. Is alcohol all you can consume?"

He forgets my drink also had cranberry juice, but I don't remind him. Or maybe I should tell him I can only consume vodka and cranberry juice, and every other thing will make my intestines dissolve into a mash of goo.

It's not the first time I've considered messing with Henry. He hangs onto my every word, or lack thereof, with reverence. To him, I am his oracle, a compass to guide him. But I am no such thing.

I need to get out of here. Henry will be thrown to whatever wolves want a piece of him. There are others like myself who hand out justice, and it will be up to them what will happen to my captor.

Unbeknownst to Henry, for now, I'm caught. The materials around me, the metal chains, stone floor, can't be manipulated for they were never alive. I'm also weakened. The events of the past few days have been too much for my system. I've spent decades roaming the world alone, observing rather than getting involved. What can I say? After millennia of existence, even beings like myself need a vacation.

I'm also not the most powerful of my kind – but not the least, thank you very much – and the energy I've expelled has been momentous. I need to recharge.

If only Henry would let me.

"Your human form," he begins, "Did you choose it? Do you have to change it once in a while?"

I can't help but smile. "It's like a hermit crab. Once this skin shell becomes too tight, I need to shed it and find another one," I tell him,

Henry looks at me with wide-eyed glee. "Really?" He asks like a child confirming his parent's promise to buy him that new toy isn't a lie. For Henry, every visit with me is Christmas morning.

"No," I say as I slump back against the wall.

Henry's growing frustrated with my behavior. As enthusiastic he is about the prospect of my granting him some sort of otherworldly power, it's not going as he imagined. Thus far, he has gained no special abilities, nor have I given him any insight into any hidden worlds. All he has earned is a snarky, immortal spirit who's becoming equally as annoyed that she has to be cornered in a loser's basement.

The best part is that the dummy has been trying to test himself.

Last night he tried to move his beer can with his mind. Deciding that it was too heavy and flat-bottomed, he next tried with a marble. Obviously, it didn't work, and all Henry did was give himself a headache from staring at a stationary object for too long.

The worst was when he wanted *me* to do it.

A few days ago, Henry brought down a bag of corn chips. He first offered them to me as a snack – hard no – and then asked me to move the bag.

Feeling particularly sassy that day – or was it night – I rocked back slightly and kicked the bag with both feet and told Henry, "there. It's moved."

Unimpressed by my display of core strength, Henry snatched the bag and stomped up the stairs like a spoiled brat. He returned an hour later with a blue plastic cup and a bottle of cheap bourbon.

Building a show of it, he made sure I watched as he poured the brown liquor into the cup. He then placed the cup in front of me, but just far enough that I wouldn't be able to reach. Not physically at least.

It was a piece of cheese in a mousetrap that I couldn't catch without getting snapped. I must admit that I was tempted even if the bourbon came out of a plastic jug and smelled of turpentine. Alcohol has an effect on this human form, one which I enjoy. It's not as strong as what actual humans feel when they imbibe, but it suffices.

But there was no way I would give Henry the satisfaction of playing his game. Also, I plain couldn't do it. I'm the queen of the dead, not a magician.

Why are humans so obsessed with telekinesis, anyway? It's as though one of the ultimate acts of power is being able to move things with your mind. I blame Carrie. Or that painfully heartwarming Matilda. Damn her.

At least it was another opportunity to screw with Henry. I pinched my face and stared at the cup, pretending to concentrate so intensely that my cheeks began to flush. After a few minutes of wobbling my head and groaning, I broke out in a snorting laugh.

You should have seen Henry! He was so on the edge of his seat watching me perform, I thought he would pass out from holding his breath. And then I started laughing. At him.

It drove him to crack. He threw the bottle of bourbon against the wall with a shout. Expecting an explosion of glass and liquor, all it did was bounce off and slide across the floor, which made the scene that much more humorous.

My laughter erupted. Henry had enough. He seized me by the throat and pressed me against the wall.

"You fucking bitch," he hissed, spit hitting my face.

His touch had no effect on me anymore. I knew what he had done, I had seen everything. His grip did hurt though. Henry dug his fingers into my neck, his palm pushing against the bones in my larynx. He was so full of rage, I thought they would break.

With a final frustrated grunt, he tossed me to the side and stood, rubbing his temples in broad circles.

"I'm sorry," he said, still angry but trying to come down. "But you make me *so* mad."

You and me both, buddy.

One thing Henry's good at is testing my resolve. That outburst makes me sincerely question whether I should leave his fate to the others or take care of him myself.

He makes my blood boil. And if I'm not careful, I'll lose control. Again.

CHAPTER 15: THE MOTHER LINKED

When Henry's not bothering me, I can enjoy the silence. Well, almost.

Technically, I'm not alone in the basement. On the other side of where I'm shackled, four bodies lie. My eyes have adjusted to the dark, and when the light's not on, I can make out their outlines.

We're always staring at each other; the four bodies and I. Henry propped each person up so that they're sitting upright against the wall. Just as I am. Except people amid rigor mortis don't sit straight, and each of the victims is positioned sloppily. One's leaning over onto another, a third has slid down to be nearly lying flat. It's a mess.

The formation reminds me of two opposing sides ready to connect on the battlefield. Except we're not at war against each other. It's quite the opposite. They want to speak to me, and with all the time we've been down here, I've listened to their stories.

The mother and her son, the two lovers taken before

they could become one. Their anguish continues beyond death, each bubbling with hunger for revenge. They want Henry to pay for his crimes. But none more than the mother.

Since the incident in the van when she touched Henry and called out to me, we've become linked. It's easier for her to communicate with me and grab my attention. Some souls are stronger than others. They have unfinished business or were taken so violently that it tainted the energy of their death, but either way, they're the loudest.

The mother begs me to set her free on Henry. But I cannot do that.

I tell her it's not my place, but she doesn't want to hear it. She won't know peace until Henry is punished, but it is not my duty to bring the dead peace. She doesn't want to hear that either.

I try and calm her, but she continues to cry. Every second of every day that I am down here, she cries.

I suppose I am not to know peace either.

CHAPTER 16: HENRY BREAKS

"HOLD STILL," Henry tells me without a hint of sarcasm. As if I can go anywhere.

In his hand, he holds a blade. It's the same bowie knife he's used for all of his killings.

"Are you trying to kill me?" I ask, leaning to the right as far as I can before feeling the tug of the metal chains keeping me up.

"No," Henry responds in the same flat tone I've been throwing at him. I must admit it's a bit funny. "Just hold still."

He pushes the blade against my cheek and pushes down, opening a slice an inch wide. It's the first time since the rest stop incident that he's had the courage to come close.

He removes the knife away which is now coated with my blood. Taking a white hand towel that's tucked into his back pocket, he mops up the fluid that's begun to flow from the side of my face. The cut isn't wide, but it is deep, and it doesn't take long for the towel to become soaked.

Henry performs all of this in a methodical stupor like a surgeon focused on his patient. I have no idea what he's doing or why he's doing it.

"What the fuck is going on?" I ask, but he says nothing. Henry wraps the bloodied knife and towel inside a plastic shopping bag and leaves.

Less than two hours later, he returns, this time without the knife or towel. Henry leans over to inspect his handiwork. Shaking his head, he's unsatisfied. The blood has dried. It's pulling my skin taught, and I feel it cracking against my cheek and down my neck where it leaked.

Henry's previous attempts to clean me were poor, and now he can't see the wound clearly through the layers.

With a scowl, Henry leaves and returns minutes later, this time with a flashlight and another, slightly cleaner towel.

When he shines the flashlight at me, he pauses. The light illuminates my irises and for a brief moment, he thinks he sees something moving within them. Shadows behind my pinprick pupils that dance like smoke.

The illusion is gone shortly after, and he continues his mission. Henry scrubs my face. The towel he brought is moistened, but not enough to break apart the dried flakes without using force. On top of that, it's a cheap towel, and besides being rough, leaves bits of white string that look like worms against meat beginning to rot.

Once the wound is visible, Henry stops scrubbing and begins analyzing. He presses on it, tries to stretch it apart with his fingers, reopening the gash in the process.

When he's finished manipulating my swollen flesh, he asks me, "Does it hurt?"

Yes, it fucking hurts, but I don't admit it. Nor do I let it show. With teeth coated in blood as if I were punched in the face, I smile.

Henry doesn't return until many hours later. This time he visits with a duffel bag. The tattered, navy blue bag looks familiar. It was the same one I saw at the rest stop. Why did Henry take it? More importantly, what's inside?

He's given up on offering me food or water, so his initial greeting doesn't include an offering of consumables. Instead, he gets right to work.

As he unzips the bag, the zipper gets caught midway on a wad of loose thread. He gives it a few strong tugs, and the force shakes whatever is inside. The items clink like metal smacking metal. It's the sound you hear when shaking a toolbox. *The Toolbox Killers*, I think. Were those the ones with the recorded tape from the podcast or were they different? What a strange time to be asking myself these questions.

The zipper becomes unstuck and slides smoothly to the end of the line. Henry reaches inside and plucks out an item. The moment he reveals the pliers, I realize what he's up to.

What a fool I've been. This entire time, I thought Henry's poking and prodding was a fear tactic, his way of trying to be intimidating so I cooperate more.

It's not. He's experimenting on me. He wants to see what I can and cannot endure and whether my powers extend into magical territories such as rapid healing.

He also wants to learn what I am made of: figuratively and literally. I'm not sure what sort of scientist Henry thinks he is, but that's not stopping him from collected samples. First, my blood. And now, something more.

The pliers are the type with a tongue and groove and Henry has to first push down my lower lip to get an idea of what width to make them. He slides the bottom piece upward so that the grip is tighter and screws it into place. Giving the pliers a few test pumps, they look like a tiny shark mouth about to bite.

I'm unsure whether to fight back or not. There's not much I can do besides thrash a few inches left and right, making it difficult for Henry to complete his extraction. But it won't stop him. On the other hand, I can sit stoically and not react, not give him the satisfaction of watching me squirm.

Always the petty one, I opt for the latter.

I sit still as Henry pinches my jaw and pushes my head against the wall to keep it steady. I sit still as he sticks his fingers in my mouth and spreads out my upper lip, his digits digging into the top of my gums. I sit still as he shoves the cold pliers into the back of my mouth and clamps down so forcefully that I'm convinced my molar will shatter before it can be separated.

Don't let him, the mother whispers. *Let me go.*

What am I supposed to do? Clenching my jaw will only do so much. He'll eventually find a way to collect my tooth, whether with a tool or repeated bashes to the face.

The root is as stubborn as I am, and it takes five yanks

to rip it free. My mouth is filled with a bitter, metallic taste from the combination of metal and blood, and I need to spit out the fluid that's building inside. I'm tempted to touch the gap with my tongue, but I think better of it.

Henry inspects the tooth that's now attached to the pliers and not my gumline. He turns it a few times, holding it up to the bulb overhead. He handles it with such care you would think it was a precious gem and not a chunk of yellowed enamel.

Not seeing anything of particular interest – the tooth looks like a tooth, shocker – Henry places the specimen inside a sandwich bag. He's upgraded from free shopping bags, and I applaud his commitment to professionalism.

As he performs his crude operation – Henry's as much of a dentist as I am an extrovert – I never break eye contact. I need him to see that I am unbothered. I also need to make sure my emotions are kept under control for my own sake.

My energy is returning, and I am becoming strong enough to act on my urges if I'm not careful. Henry's keeping me subdued with physical pain, but that does nothing to keep me weakened.

It's psychic pain that sedates me. And being trapped with four restless souls has hardened me once again.

Let me go.

BOULDER COUNTY POLICE DEPARTMENT

Boulder, Colorado

PRESS RELEASE

The Boulder County Police Department is asking the community for tips and information leading to the identification of the person or persons responsible for the disappearances of Deborah Jones (45) and Justin Jones (13). CCTV cameras captured an automobile that was parked next to both Dave's Diner and the South Boulder Trail where Deborah and Justin were last seen. The van, which has Colorado license plates, appears to be a vintage Chevrolet G20 converter van ranging from 1986-1989. It is tan in color with darker brown stripes. Anyone with information is asked to immediately call 911.

CHAPTER 18: LET GO

AND SO IT goes like this for days.

Henry comes down with his bag of tools and takes pieces. First a few teeth, more chunks of my flesh, fingernails, and extra blood samples. Then he begins to elevate his endeavors.

Small bits of my body are not enough, and Henry decides to take more substantial samples.

It starts with a toe. He takes the pinky one which I suppose is kind of him since it's the least important for my ability to walk. Then comes a finger, then another. He would take an entire limb if he could figure out another way to keep me bound.

He never takes the thumbs. Without those, I might be able to slide out.

Throughout what's become the world's slowest autopsy, I have kept calm. On the outside at least.

With each extraction, Henry removes a part of my body and also my willpower. Unbeknownst to him, he's removing the bricks that are keeping the darkness within me sealed. The levy is soon to break if he doesn't stop.

Don't let him! The mother insists. She's been talking a lot.

Henry, on the other hand, says nothing as he operates. Now that I think about it, he hasn't spoken for days. He and I have settled into a silent rhythm. He is focused on his work and I on my attempts to maintain tranquility.

When Henry is finished with the session, he returns upstairs, making sure to take his belongings with him. I'm becoming less physically able to move, but he still doesn't trust me near anything pointed or sharp.

Let me go.

Above me, Henry continues the second part of his analyses. There's not much he can do clinically, so he's had to become inventive.

The blood doesn't do much. It dries the same and has the same coloration. None of the tests Henry bought at Walgreens work. He checks my cholesterol, HIV status, blood type, even food sensitivity, and they all return inconclusive.

The teeth follow a similar pattern.

He broke open my first tooth with a hammer. Its interior looked like any other tooth. Layers of pulp and dentin wrapped in a hard enamel shell. Since that tooth was ruined, he pulled another. There wasn't much he could do the intact one, so it sat there. Maybe he would try and plant it like a seed. Henry *is* that clueless, after all.

Unhappy with the results, Henry attempts other avenues.

Sitting in his dining room, he examines the display before him. No one visits him and his home is off-the-grid, so there's little chance of being caught with a spread of bloodied human parts.

Henry's also given up in his attempts to be subtle. No longer concerned that he will be apprehended, he's become relaxed. He thinks he's immune to the laws created by man, that he's become above them. It's a false sense of security since nothing has changed. He has no new special powers or immortality, but Henry has convinced himself otherwise.

In his defense, no authorities are searching for him. Even through his bumbling, he's managed to evade notice. His four victims are officially classified as missing persons, but they're too spread out and too random to form a link.

Henry's lucked out, and now he can lose his mind in peace.

A strip of flesh, the length of an earthworm, lays before him atop a page torn from a circular ad. He pinches the top of the skin and peels it off. It clings to the paper, and as he pries, pieces of the weekly ad get glued on. Ironically, it's mostly an image of a chuck roast that's on sale for $2.99 per pound.

He holds up the strand of meat, wiggling it to test its density. It's begun to brown at the ends, and Henry considers trimming the piece first. Changing his mind and deciding it would be best to keep the sample whole – scientific integrity at its best – he opens his mouth and inserts the meat.

It's rubbery and tough, difficult to chew. He gets in a

few bites before swallowing the rest whole. Afraid it will get lodged; he washes it down with a chug of Coors Light and a bite of ham sandwich to cleanse the palette.

Henry's not afraid to die. He believes himself to be immortal. But he is afraid of discomfort, and, unless you're Ed Gein, having a spongy piece of human skin caught in your throat isn't a fun time.

Leaning back in his pine chair, its joints creaking, Henry waits. What he's waiting for, he doesn't know, but he's hoping for an effect. If I won't share my powers with him, the next obvious answer is ingesting my essence. Or so he believes.

In reality, Henry's just being a cannibal. No more, no less. The most he'll get out of this game is a stomachache.

"Fuck!" Henry shouts, throwing his beer can against the wall. Tossing alcoholic drinks has become his preferred reaction to stress. It's replaced the lip biting.

The beer can fizzles as honey-colored liquid pours onto the carpet. Henry doesn't move to clean it up. Why bother? The house is a mess, and nothing has been working.

Henry rushes into the basement, mouth-frothing.

"What more do you want from me?!" He yells. "I've done everything you've asked! You promised me I would be rewarded. Why won't you fucking deliver!"

Henry shakes my shoulders as he hollers in my face. I flop like a ragdoll, physically drained from the abuse.

I've become no more than a lump on the ground. My body stained with splotches of crimson brown, my muscles weak and limp and unable to sit upright any longer. Between the corpses that have been rotting for weeks and my wounds both new and old, the basement is beginning to smell like a nineteenth-century slaughterhouse.

"I told you before," I say, trying not to whistle through missing teeth. "I am not the one."

Henry lets go.

He paces around the room in a circle like a tiger at the zoo. "It's a test," he says out loud though he's talking to himself. "This is a test. You want to see whether I am worthy."

Henry kneels before me in an act of penance, his fingers locking together. "I am *so* sorry. I'll try harder to prove to you that I am deserving. I believe in you, in your gifts. You are my savior," he pleads.

It's at that moment, when I see Henry praying before a false god, that I hate him more than I have before. He's so pathetic to think that I would have pity on him, this worthless creature.

LET ME GO! the mother bellows, and I no longer hold onto my control. Nor do I want to.

Henry needs to suffer for his sins. He needs to go to his final judgment. And I have decided it will be me who delivers him.

I can hold back no longer. Between the mother's pain and the agony Henry has put my physical body through, I am weak. I have maintained the levy long enough, but the pressures of the incoming tidal wave are too much to bear. I must let go.

"You are free," I say. Henry thinks it's for him, and he smiles.

Sounds of shuffling begin behind him. They're

labored and make a grinding sound like bone against bone.

He hears the gliding of bodies against stone and turns. The four are reanimating. It's messy and uncoordinated, their movements irregular. Each limb bends independently of the other in broken motions, resembling marionettes being puppeteer by an amateur.

The dead are dancing.

It's the mother who leads. She claws toward Henry with rapid speed, slamming her stiffened palms against the floor and using her knees to crawl.

Slam, slide, *slam,* slide, *slam,* slide.

She's practically running on her belly, and before Henry can fathom what's happening, she's on top of him. Her palms now slam against his body as she grabs for purchase. Any piece of him she can clutch with her fingers, she tears away.

The impact of her actions makes her softened skin burst open like a wet newspaper, but she doesn't stop. The bones beneath are sharper and work even better to tear at Henry, which she uses to her advantage.

Henry can't hear her speak, but I can. She laughs, and screams, and cries, cursing Henry for taking her son and reveling in her revenge.

Henry's no match for her attacks. Each blow he delivers lands hollow. The dead cannot feel bodily pain.

One punch connects with her shoulder and is enough to send her backward. She's disconnected from him for a moment, but it's not long before the others have caught up.

Each victim has their own axe to grind, and each

takes out their vendettas with a crazed fury. Chunks of skin, both decomposed and new, fly into the air like organic confetti.

The display is fitting. It *is* a celebration, after all.

I watch with delight as the four collect their pounds of flesh. I can feel their relief. They're in the midst of completing their final task before moving on. And based on what I've learned, they're all worthy of paradise.

There's one final task for me as well. I'm still shackled to the wall, and without outside intervention, I'll be grounded here for ages.

The mother senses my dilemma. Henry has stopped whimpering long ago, and she is fulfilled. Her mouth and hands have become no more than broken shards of browned bone, but they'll do the trick.

Slithering toward me, she wedges herself between me and the wall and begins to chew.

As grueling as it feels, it is not an act of animosity. She's not trying to hurt me; she's trying to thank me.

The forearm goes first. It's the thinnest with less substance to drill through. The bone is the hardest part, but she's able to crack it with a few bites.

The chain falls to the ground with a *clank*, and I am able to free both of my arms. The mother has begun to descend on my calf, but I let her know there's no need. The chains are connected, and now that one half has been removed, I can slide the end through the metal loop, and release my legs.

I give the mother a nod. Our time together is over, and she's clear to watch her son eat away at Henry. With what's left of her jaw, she smiles.

Henry's dead. He'll be sent to his final judgment which I know, based on his history, won't result in bliss.

I shouldn't have caused his death, but I don't regret it. Maybe I'll face consequences for my actions, maybe I won't, it's always a gamble whether someone's paying attention.

One thing I know for sure is whatever was communicating with Henry will be upset. It will be coming for me next.

As I hobble out of Henry's front door, the sounds of shattered mouths grinding behind me, I feel terrific, warm. Almost giddy.

Whenever it comes, I'll be ready for a fight.

ACKNOWLEDGMENTS

First of all, a big thank you to Sam Richard who believed in this story from the start and taught me a lot about the industry.

A big thanks to the following people: Babcia and Dziadek, Samantha Coppola, Robert Goodman, Christine Alexy, Rebecca Kallemyn, The Langs, and Stephanie Bense.

Another thank you to my parents for instilling the love of horror at a very early age and making me the wonderful weirdo I am today.

A final thank you to Steve who is continuously a support no matter what idea pops into my head.

ABOUT THE AUTHOR

Maria Abrams is a horror writer and graphic designer.
She currently lives in Colorado with her two rescue dogs
and one life-size Chucky doll.
Find her online at www.abramstheauthor.com and
Twitter @AbramsWriter.

Beautiful/Grotesque - Edited by Sam Richard

Five authors of strange fiction, Roland Blackburn (*Seventeen Names For Skin*), Jo Quenell (*The Mud Ballad*), Katy Michelle Quinn (*Girl in the Walls*), Joanna Koch (*The Wingspan of Severed Hands*), and Sam Richard (*Sabbath of the Fox-Devils*) each bring you their own unique vision of the macabre and the glorious violently colliding. From full-on hardcore horror, to decadently surreal nightmares, and noir-fueled psychosis, to an eerie meditation on grief, and familial quiet horror, *Beautiful/Grotesque* guides us through the murky waters where the monstrous and the breathtaking meet.

The Wingspan of Severed Hands by Joanna Koch

Three Women, One Battle. A world gone mad. Cities abandoned. Dreams invade waking minds. An invisible threat lures those who oppose its otherworldly violence to become acolytes of a nameless cult. As a teenage girl struggles for autonomy, a female weapons director in a secret research facility develops a living neuro-cognitive device that explodes into self-awareness. Discovering their hidden emotional bonds, all three unveil a common enemy through dissonant realities that intertwine in a cosmic battle across hallucinatory dreamscapes. Time is the winning predator, and every moment spirals deeper into the heart of the beast.

Seventeen Names for Skin by Roland Blackburn

After a cancer diagnosis gives her six-months to live, Snow Turner does what any introverted body-piercer might: hire a dark-web assassin and take out a massive life insurance policy to help her ailing father. But when a vicious attack leaves her all too alive and with a polymorphic curse, the bodies begin stacking up. As the insatiable hunger and violent changes threaten to consumer her, she learns that someone may still be trying to end her life. Can Snow keep her humanity intact, or will she tear everything she loves apart?